5810 J

HAILSTONES AND
HALIBUT BONES

Adventures in Colour

HAILSTONES AND HALIBUT BONES

Adventures in Colour

MARY O'NEILL

Illustrated by Leonard Weisgard

A WORLD'S WORK CHILDREN'S BOOK

Copyright © 1961 by Mary Gibbons O'Neill
Illustrations Copyright © 1961 by Leonard Weisgard
All Rights Reserved
First published in Great Britain 1962 by
World's Work Ltd
The Windmill Press, Kingswood, Tadworth, Surrey
Sixth impression 1972

Printed by offset in Great Britain by
William Clowes & Sons, Limited
London, Beccles and Colchester

SBN 437 64700 5

Like acrobats on a high trapeze
The Colours pose and bend their knees
Twist and turn and leap and blend
Into shapes and feelings without end...

WHAT IS PURPLE?

Time is purple
Just before night
When most people
Turn on the light——
But if you don't it's
A beautiful sight.
Asters are purple,
There's purple ink.
Purple's more popular
Than you think. . . .
It's sort of a great
Grandmother to pink.
There are purple shadows
And purple veils,
Some ladies purple
Their fingernails.

There's purple jam
And purple jell
And a purple bruise
Next day will tell
Where you landed
When you fell.
The purple feeling
Is rather put-out
The purple look is a
Definite pout.
But the purple sound
Is the loveliest thing
It's a violet opening
In the spring.

WHAT IS GOLD?

Gold is a metal
Gold is a ring
Gold is a very
Beautiful thing.
Gold is the sunshine
Light and thin
Warm as a muffin
On your skin.
Gold is the moon
Gold are the stars;
Jupiter, Venus
Saturn and Mars,

Gold is the colour of
Clover honey
Gold is a certain
Kind of money.
Gold is alive
In a flickering fish
That lives its life
In a crystal dish.
Gold is the answer
To many a wish.
Gold is feeling
Like a king
It's like having the most
Of everything——
Long time ago
I was told
Yellow's mother's name
Is gold. . . .

WHAT IS BLACK?

Black is the night
When there isn't a star
And you can't tell by looking
Where you are.
Black is a pail of paving tar.
Black is jet
And things you'd like to forget.
Black is a chimney
Black is a cat,
A leopard, a raven,
A silk top hat.
The sound of black is
"Boom! Boom! Boom!"
Echoing in
An empty room.
Black is kind——

It covers up
The shabby street,
The broken cup.
Black is the coal
That drives a train
The soot spots on
The window pane.
Black is a feeling
Hard to explain
Like suffering but
Without the pain.
Black is liquorice
And patent leather shoes
Black is the print
In the news.
Black is beauty
In its deepest form,
The darkest cloud
In a thunderstorm.
Think of what starlight
And lamplight would lack
Diamonds and fireflies
If they couldn't lean against
Black. . . .

WHAT IS BROWN?

Brown is the colour of a country road
Back of a tortoise
Back of a toad.
Brown is cinnamon
And morning toast
And the good smell of
The Sunday roast.
Brown is the colour of work
And the sound of a river,
Brown is bronze and a bow
And a quiver.
Brown is the house
On the edge of town
Where wind is tearing
The fences down.

Brown is a freckle
Brown is a mole
Brown is the earth
When you dig a hole.
Brown is the hair
On many a head
Brown is chocolate
And gingerbread.
Brown is a feeling
You get inside
When wondering makes
Your mind grow wide.
Brown is a leather shoe
And a good glove——
Brown is as comfortable
As love.

WHAT IS BLUE?

Blue is the colour of the sky
Without a cloud
Cool, distant, beautiful
And proud.
Blue is the quiet sea
And the eyes of some people,
And many agree
As they grow older and older
Blue is the scarf
Spring wears on her shoulder.
Blue is twilight,
Shadows on snow,
Blue is feeling
Sad and low.

Blue is a lake,
A sapphire ring,
You can smell blue
In many a thing:
Lupin and larkspur
Forget-me-nots, too.
And if you listen
You can hear blue
In wind over water
And wherever flax blooms
And when evening steps into
Lonely rooms.
Cold is blue:
Flame shot from a welding torch
Is, too:
Hot, wild, screaming, blistering Blue—
And on winter mornings
The dawns are blue. . . .

WHAT IS GREY?

Grey is the colour of an elephant
And a mouse
And a tumble-down house.
It's fog and smog,
And very fine print,
It's a hush and
The wetness of melting slush.
Tiredness and oysters
Both are grey,

Smoke swirls
And grandmother's curls.
So are some spring coats
And nanny-goats.
Pigeons are grey
And a rainy day
The sad look of a slum
And chewing gum.
Pussy willows are grey
In a velvety way.
Suits, shoes
And bad news,
Beggars' hats
And alley cats
Skin of a mole
And a worn slipper sole.
Content is grey
And sleepiness, too
They wear grey suede gloves
When they're touching you. . . .

WHAT IS WHITE?

White is a dove
And lily of the valley
And a puddle of milk
Spilled in an alley——
A ship's sail
A kite's tail
A wedding veil
Hailstones and
Halibut bones
And some people's
Telephones.
The hottest and most blinding light
Is white.
And breath is white
When you blow it out on a frosty night.
White is the shining absence of all colour
Then absence is white
Out of touch
Out of sight.

White is marshmallow
And vanilla ice cream
And the part you can't remember
In a dream.
White is the sound
Of a light foot walking
White is a pair of
Whispers talking.
White is the beautiful
Broken lace
Of snowflakes falling
On your face.
You can smell white
In a country room
Near the end of May
When the cherries bloom.

38

WHAT IS ORANGE?

Orange is a tiger lily,
A carrot,
A feather from
A parrot,
A flame,
The wildest colour
You can name.
Orange is a happy day
Saying good-bye
In a sunset that
Shocks the sky.
Orange is brave
Orange is bold
It's bittersweet
And marigold.

Orange is zip
Orange is dash
The brightest stripe
In a party sash.
Orange is an orange
Also a mango
Orange is music
Of the tango.
Orange is the fur
Of the fiery fox,
The brightest crayon
In the box.
And in the autumn
When leaves are turning
Orange is the smell
Of a bonfire burning. . . .

WHAT IS RED?

Red is a sunset
Blazing and bright.
Red is feeling brave
With all your might.
Red is a sunburn
Spot on your nose,
Sometimes red
Is a red, red rose.
Red squiggles out
When you cut your hand.
Red is a brick and
The sound of a band.
Red is a hotness
You get inside
When you're embarrassed
And want to hide.

Fire-cracker, fire-engine
Fire-flicker red——
And when you're angry
Red runs through your head.
Red is an Indian,
A Valentine heart,
The trimming on
A circus cart.
Red is a lipstick,
Red is a shout,
Red is a signal
That says: "Watch out!"
Red is a great big
Rubber ball.
Red is the giant-est
Colour of all.
Red is a show-off
No doubt about it——
But can you imagine
Living without it?

WHAT IS PINK?

Pink is the colour of a rose.
They come in other colours
But everyone knows
Pink is the mother-colour of a rose.
Pink is a new baby,
The inside of a shell.
Pink is a cooked shrimp
And a canterbury bell.

Pink is blossom
Gauzy . . . frail
The wind's exquisite
Wedding veil.
Pink is a bonbon,
Pink is a blush,
Some Easter bunnies
Are pink plush.
If you stand in an orchard
In the middle of Spring
And you don't make a sound
You can hear pink sing,
A darling, whispery
Song of a thing.

Pink is the beautiful
Little sister of red
My teacher said,
And the ribbon a girl ties
Round her head.
Pink is the sash
With the lovely fold
You'll remember
When you're old.
Pink is the flower
On a lady's hat
That nods and bows
This way and that.

WHAT IS GREEN?

Green is the grass
And the leaves of trees
Green is the smell
Of a country breeze.
Green is lettuce
And sometimes the sea.
When green is a feeling
You pronounce it N–V.
Green is a coolness
You get in the shade
Of the tall old woods
Where the moss is made.

Green is a flutter
That comes in Spring
When frost melts out
Of everything.
Green is a grasshopper
Green is jade
Green is hiding
In the shade——
Green is an olive
And a pickle.
The sound of green
Is a water-trickle
Green is the world
After the rain
Bathed and beautiful
Again.

April is green
Peppermint, too.
Every elf has
One green shoe.
Under a grape ~~arbour~~ vine
Air is green
With sprinkles of sunlight
In between.
Green is the meadow,
Green is the fuzz
That covers up
Where winter was.
Green is ivy and
Honeysuckle vine.
Green is yours
Green is mine. . . .

WHAT IS YELLOW?

Yellow is the colour of the sun
The feeling of fun
The yolk of an egg
A duck's bill
A canary bird
And a daffodil.
Yellow's sweet corn
Ripe oats
Hummingbirds'
Little throats
Lemon squash and
Chinese silk
The cream on top
Of Jersey milk
Dandelions and
Daisy hearts
Custard pies and
Lemon tarts.

Yellow blinks
On summer nights
In the off-and-on of
Firefly lights.
Yellow's a topaz,
A candle flame.
Felicity's a
Yellow name.
Yellow's mimosa,
And I guess,
Yellow's the colour of
Happiness.

The Colours live
Between black and white
In a land that we
Know best by sight.
But knowing best
Isn't everything,
For colours dance
And colours sing,
And colours laugh
And colours cry—
Turn off the light
And colours die,
And they make you feel
Every feeling there is
From the grumpiest grump
To the fizziest fizz.
And you and you and I
Know well
Each has a taste
And each has a smell
And each has a wonderful
Story to tell....